Crystal's QUEST

AN ADVENTURE INTO THE WORLD OF GEMSTONES

LISA FONTANELLA

Illustrations by Tam Veilleux

Publisher's Cataloging-In-Publication Data
(Prepared by The Donohue Group, Inc.)

Names: Fontanella, Lisa, author. | Veilleux, Tam, illustrator.
Title: Crystal's quest : an adventure into the world of gemstones / Lisa Fontanella ; illustrations by Tam Veilleux.
Description: [Seattle, Washington] : KDP Amazon, [2019] | Interest age level: 007-011. | Summary: "Each chapter is a story about friendship, emotions and the amazing properties of gemstones. The stories revolve around Crystal and her beagle buddy, Noodle, and all the characters they meet"–Provided by publisher.
Identifiers: ISBN 9781641840798 (paperback) | ISBN 9781641840804 (ebook)
Subjects: LCSH: Precious stones–Juvenile fiction. | Friendship–Juvenile fiction. | Geology–Juvenile fiction. | CYAC: Precious stones–Fiction. | Friendship–Fiction. | Geology–Fiction.
Classification: LCC PZ7.1.F656 Cr 2019 (print) | LCC PZ7.1.F656 (ebook) | DDC [Fic]–dc23

Published by Lisa Fontanella / IngramSpark
Edited by Susan Puiia
Illustrations By Tam Veilleux
Design by Kendra Cagle, 5 Lakes Design

www.LisaFontanella.com

FOR
Gunny

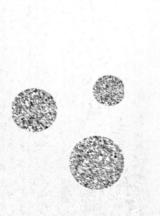

Acknowledgements

I am so grateful for all the support from
family and friends. You all ROCK!

Tam, thank you so much for your fabulous illustrations!
You truly made all the characters come to life.

Susie, I appreciate your sentence
structure and the support!

Kendra, what a marvel you are. You embraced
my vision and ran with it. Awesome!

Crystal

Loves rocks and
her dog Noodle.

Noodle

Adores Crystal
and hates peas.

Grandpa Dan

He and Crystal
enjoy finding and
learning about rocks.

Nathan

Crystal's friend
and big sports fan.

Rocks are fun

Different cultures all over the world have
loved rocks for many, many years!

Rocks have different features:

MULTIPLE COLORS
GLITTERY
ONE COLOR
SMOOTH
ROUGH

All shapes and sizes.

All through history, rocks have
been used to make people feel better.

Rocks can help you be:

HAPPY
CONFIDENT
CALM
CREATIVE
PATIENT

I love having rocks in my pocket.
I like the feel of them in my hand.

1
Chapter

GRANDPA DAN'S FRIEND

As the morning ☀ SUN streamed through her window, Crystal slowly opened her eyes to greet the day. She sat up and noticed a purple letter on her dresser. Yawning, she rubbed her eyes and went over to read it. The cryptic letter was from Grandpa Dan and all it said was,

Go to my favorite fishing spot. My friend will be waiting there for you.

Love, Grandpa Dan
P.S. Bring grapes

Bring GRAPES? 🍇 Crystal read the letter twice for she was sure she misread Grandpa Dan's squiggly handwriting. They aren't kidding when they say doctors have horrible handwriting. Grandpa Dan's is the worst!

Just as she finished reading the mysterious letter,
Noodle came bounding in with a happy beagle face and slurpy
kisses for his favorite person, Crystal.

"Looks like we're going on a QUEST,"
she said to Noodle.

Noodle was beside himself with EXCITEMENT.
When Noodle gets excited, he does a 'beagle boogie' where
he dances around in circles, puts one front paw up, then
shifts and lifts the other paw. His final dance move is to get
up on his hind legs and wiggle. His tail wags so hard it
looks like it could come off at any minute!

Crystal and Noodle ate breakfast. Actually, Crystal ate her breakfast while Noodle SNARFED his down in two gulps. Noodle loves food and will eat anything except peas. Noodle HATES peas!

As Crystal and Noodle were getting ready to head out the door, Crystal's mother said,

"Better wear a jacket.
The weather is chilly outside."

This made Crystal quite happy as she got to wear her favorite fleece jacket (purple, of course). Purple is Crystal's favorite color. At least it is this week. Last week her favorite color was blue.

"I put a bag together
to take on your quest,"

Crystal's mother said.

"Have FUN!"

Crystal took the shopping bag from the kitchen counter and said, "Thanks, Mom." Crystal gave her mother a kiss on the cheek, and she and Noodle headed out the door.

It normally wasn't a long distance to Grandpa Dan's favorite fishing spot, but today the walk took a lot longer. Noodle stopped to *sniff* and investigate absolutely everything! Finally they got to the dirt road that runs along the river. As they walked, Crystal could hear a **noise** behind her, but every time she turned around, she didn't see anything. Approaching the river bank, Crystal settled on a big rock with Noodle climbing up beside her.

As they waited to meet Grandpa Dan's mysterious friend, Crystal searched the ground looking for rocks to add to her very large collection. Every time Grandpa Dan comes home from a trip, he brings Crystal a rock. Grandpa Dan and Crystal share a L♥VE of rocks and enjoy learning all about them.

Crystal spotted an interesting white rock and put it in her pocket. (Crystal ALWAYS has rocks in her pocket.) Surprised, she pulled another purple note from her pocket.

"Look! Another note from Grandpa Dan!"

The note instructed Crystal to put two grapes on the
ground and wait for his friend Gertie to arrive.
Grandpa Dan wrote,

"GERTIE NEEDS
TO LEARN ABOUT
GENEROSITY.
GERTIE'S ROCK
IS IN THE BAG."

Crystal and Noodle looked at each other totally
CONFUSED!

Crystal followed the note's INSTRUCTION and reached
into the bag for two red grapes. She placed the grapes on
the ground and turned to Noodle and said,

"I guess now we wait for Grandpa
Dan's friend to arrive."

Just as Crystal finished her sentence, she heard a noise
from behind the big rock. Crystal and Noodle peeked
around the rock and came face to face with a bird.
Crystal and the bird screamed at the same time,

"EEEK!"

"Are you Gertie?"

Crystal asked. Gertie ignored the question and *ran* straight to the grapes. Crystal and Noodle couldn't believe their eyes. Gertie eats even *faster* than Noodle! The grapes were *gone* in seconds and Gertie did not look pleased.

"I want more grapes!"

Gertie demanded. Crystal reached in the bag and put two more red grapes on the ground. The grapes vanished. Crystal put more grapes on the ground. The grapes VANISHED.

Watching Gertie eat all those grapes made Noodle hungry. Noodle saw two grapes on the ground and started moving toward them. Seeing what Noodle was planning to do, Gertie dived for the grapes and reached them before Noodle. SNARF. Gertie was upset. Her face was red and she tried to YELL at Noodle, but she had so many grapes in her mouth, nobody could understand what she was saying.

Taking the opportunity to talk to Gertie while she
was still eating the grapes, Crystal said,

"Gertie, you ate almost all the
grapes, and it's okay to share
so others can have some.
Don't you want to
SHARE them?"

Now Gertie was frantically flapping her wings trying to
shoo Noodle away. Crystal now understood what Grandpa
Dan meant in his note. Gertie does not like to share! Crystal
wondered what rock Grandpa Dan chose for Gertie.

Crystal reached in the shopping bag and pulled out a
beautiful pink rhodonite rock. A big smile came
across Crystal's face because she knows that this rock
helps someone be kind, generous, and to get along
with others.

Gertie was getting tired of flapping, and she was almost finished eating the grapes. She sat down and POUTED.

Crystal sat near Gertie (not too close) and said,

"I have a 🎁 PRESENT from my grandfather, your friend."

Crystal put the rock on the ground and 🛑STOPPED Gertie just before she ate it. Crystal explained,

"Grandpa Dan chose this rock just for you, Gertie. We want you to have it."

Gertie didn't know what to do. She looked pleased and confused. Crystal wondered if Gertie had ever been given a present before. Crystal felt more COMPASSION for Gertie.

As Crystal and Noodle started walking away, Crystal turned to look back at Gertie. She wasn't sure, but she thought Gertie was smiling.

GERTIE THE GROUSE

When Grandpa Dan said we would meet his friend,
I had no idea he was talking about a bird! I called
Grandpa Dan and told him we met Gertie and how
she got mad at Noodle. Grandpa Dan laughed when
he heard that. Gertie has been visiting Grandpa
Dan every time he goes to the river and they have
become friends. Grandpa Dan explained that Gertie
didn't have any friends or family, so she never
learned how to share.

At first, I thought Gertie was mean, but it turns
out she didn't know how to be friends. The next
time Grandpa Dan goes to visit Gertie, I'll go with
him. I may have to convince Noodle to come! I will
always be grateful to Gertie for eating the grapes
before Noodle ate them. Grapes are very bad for
dogs to eat!

I've been with Grandpa Dan many times when
he has given a rock to someone who needs it.
Grandpa Dan knows a lot about rocks! We learn
about rocks by reading geology books...

Crystal's Journal

and looking for information on the computer. Grandpa Dan says that rocks have energy. He explained that rocks have certain traits that make them special. It's like each rock has its own personality. When I pick up a rock, I just know when it is the right one for me! There must be a lot of 'right' rocks for me because I have a LOT of rocks!!!

MY THOUGHT FOR TODAY!
I wonder what it would be like to always see the good in people. Any time I doubt that, I let my doubt go!

Rhodonite

HOW YOU SAY IT:
Row-don-ite

GEOLOGY FUN FACT

Geology is the study of rocks. People who study geology are called geologists.

Rocks are used to make cars, video games, aluminum baseball bats, airplanes, and jewelry.

RHODONITE GEOGRAPHY

Rhodonite is found in many areas in the world but was first found in the Ural Mountains of Russia. Russia is the largest country in the world. It has shorelines on three oceans (the Atlantic, Pacific, and Arctic).

People used to call rhodonite the 'eagle stone' because eagles would bring small pieces to their nests.

RHODONITE HISTORY

Rhodonite was a very popular stone in Russia. It was used to carve items such as bowls and sculptures for famous and important people.

WHAT DO I DO WITH MY ROCK?

Put it in your pocket, in your room, in your hand.

USE RHODONITE WHEN YOU WANT TO:

give and receive kindness,
be more generous,
get along with others.

Rhodonite became the official gemstone of Massachusetts in 1979.

Rhodonite

KINDNESS

GENEROSITY

COOPERATION

Crystal's Quest

To order a copy,
go to **LisaFontanella.com**
or **Amazon.com**

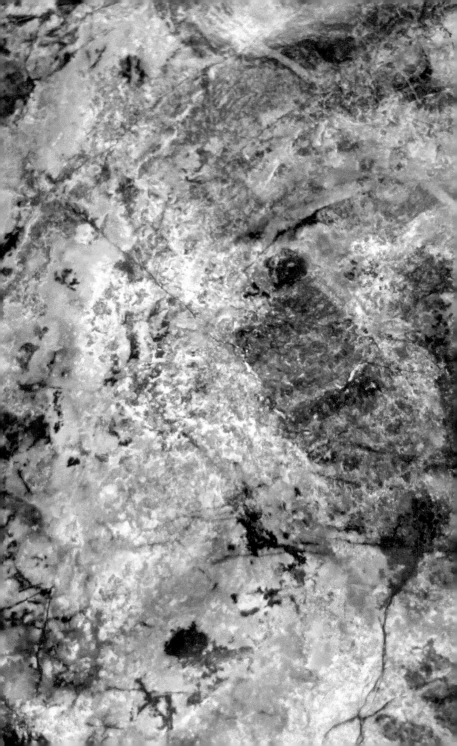

Chapter 2

SING!

Crystal bound out of bed, EXCITED to see Grandpa Dan's next letter. Noodle heard her getting up and ran full speed into her bedroom, sliding across the floor and almost crashing into her.

"Let's see what adventure Grandpa Dan has for us today," Crystal said to Noodle.

They both looked around the room, but there was no purple letter. Crystal and Noodle searched the house but they could not locate the note. Puzzled, Crystal plopped down on a kitchen chair.

"Where could it be?"

she thought out loud. She glanced down and saw the purple letter on top of the newspaper. As she picked up the letter, she noticed a newspaper ad for the animal adoption center just down the road. Of course! She and Grandpa Dan love to go visit the animals.

Crystal opened up the letter.

Go to the very back of the adoption center. Someone there needs ENCOURAGEMENT. Give them this rock.

Love, Grandpa Dan

Crystal rushed to get dressed, making sure she put the rock in her pocket before her and Noodle headed out the door.

Crystal knew that Noodle was quite excited about where they were going because he didn't 🛑STOP every two feet to sniff something! It was a quick walk to the animal adoption center and no time at all when Crystal and Noodle walked through the front gate.

They were greeted by Andrew, a red-headed staff member who wore a bright ORANGE shirt with animals all over it. "Hello, Andrew," Crystal and Noodle said together. Andrew was always happy to see Crystal and Noodle.

The adoption center is a wonderful place where all kinds of animals can find a good  HOME. Grandpa Dan volunteers there and sometimes Crystal goes with him.

Crystal and Noodle walked through the center, stopping to say **hello** to some of the animals. Ezra the hamster waved enthusiastically,

"Hello there, my friends.
What a beautiful day!"

Ezra is always in a good mood.

When they got to the back of the center, Crystal and Noodle looked around to see who Grandpa Dan wanted them to meet.

SUDDENLY...

lively music started playing. Noodle just L♥VES music! He excitedly ran in the direction of the music with a happy beagle face and a wagging tail. Then Crystal and Noodle heard a very loud, "SQUAWK! SQUEEK!" Noodle put his paws over his ears to block out the loud singing. They looked up and saw a beautiful, green parrot singing and dancing to the music. He was having so much fun!

When the parrot saw someone watching him, he abruptly closed his beak. He hung his head and did not look at Crystal and Noodle. Crystal said,

"That was AWESOME! You are a good dancer and your singing is, well, enthusiastic. We'd love to hear you sing and dance to another song."

The parrot would not look up. The parrot was silent. It was a few minutes before he finally spoke and said,

"I don't like to sing in front of people. I was told I'm not very good, and I sing REALLY

LOUD."

"Who cares what people think? You love to sing, so you should sing,"

Crystal told him.

"All you need is some
CONFIDENCE."

Crystal reached into her pocket and pulled out the rock
that Grandpa Dan chose. The blue and green rock called
chrysocolla was the perfect rock for the parrot!

"This will help you be more
confident and BRAVE,

Crystal said, as she put the rock on the parrot's wing.

Crystal wasn't sure what else to say to
ENCOURAGE the parrot, but Noodle had an idea.
All of a sudden, Noodle burst into song.

"AHH – oooo! AHH –oooo! AHH – oooo!"

Squawk slowly lifted his head and started to sing quietly.
As Noodle continued, the parrot sang louder and louder.
Noodle and the parrot were singing a DUET.
A very loud duet!

When the song ended, Crystal clapped
enthusiastically. But she was not the only
person clapping. Crystal looked over and saw Mrs. Jackson
smiling and clapping too. Both Squawk and Noodle took a
BOW with big smiles on their faces.

"Hi, Mrs. Jackson.
It's nice to see you again,"

Crystal said. Mrs. Jackson didn't answer her.
Crystal repeated her greeting, but
Mrs. Jackson still didn't answer.

Then Mrs. Jackson noticed Crystal
looking at her and said,

"I'm sorry,
dear. I had my
hearing aid
turned down,
and I didn't hear
you talking to
me. They were
WONDERFUL..."

...Mrs. Jackson said, looking
at the parrot and Noodle.

"What is your name?" Mrs. Jackson asked the parrot.
"SQUAWK." the parrot replied.

"Would you like to come
live with me, Squawk?"

Mrs. Jackson asked. The parrot couldn't believe it!

"You want to adopt me?" the parrot asked,
surprised. "Are you sure? I'm very loud."

Mrs. Jackson smiled at Crystal and said,

"That won't be a problem. I'd L♥VE to
have you come live with me."

The parrot let out a huge SQUAWK and
began to happy dance!

Crystal and Noodle said goodbye and walked to the other
end of the adoption center where they could easily
hear Squawk singing.

"I'm going home."

What an AWESOME day!

SQUAWK THE PARROT

Noodle is still singing the song he and Squawk sang together. I imagine Squawk is still singing too. I smile when I think about how Squawk gained his confidence, bravely opened his beak, and burst into song. He was so full of joy when he sang. He couldn't contain his excitement (and neither could Noodle!) ☺ And what awesome dancing!

Grandpa Dan and I have gone to visit the animals at the animal adoption center many times before, and I had the same feeling as I always do. I want to adopt ALL the animals (even the cats, but I won't tell Noodle that). I'm so glad Squawk now has a home and can do what he loves.

MY THOUGHT FOR TODAY!
I wonder what it would be like to always encourage people. Any time I doubt that, I let my doubt go!

Chrysocolla

HOW YOU SAY IT:

Chris-OH-cola

Chrysocolla

CREATIVITY

CONFIDENCE

BRAVERY

GEOLOGY FUN FACT

The oldest rocks on Earth are 4 billion years old. That's 4,000,000,000! That's a lot of zeroes!!

CHRYSOCOLLA GEOGRAPHY

The blue and green colors of chrysocolla look like the earth's surface from space.

Chrysocolla is found in many areas of the world, including Chile. Chile is a long country that stretches down the west coast of South America. The official language of Chile is Spanish.

CHRYSOCOLLA HISTORY

In ancient Egypt, chrysocolla was called the "wise stone" because it helped enemies talk and live in peace.

Cleopatra was a ruler of ancient Egypt. Part of her job was to be a peacekeeper, making sure that everyone got along. Cleopatra wore chrysocolla jewelry everywhere she went.

WHAT DO I DO WITH MY ROCK?

Put it in your pocket, in your room, in your hand.

USE CHRYSOCOLLA WHEN YOU WANT TO:

be more creative,
be more confident,
be braver.

Chrysocolla is the national stone of Israel.

Crystal's Quest

To order a copy,
go to **LisaFontanella.com**
or **Amazon.com**

3
Chapter

A MOO-VING TALE

Another day! Another quest! On this day, Grandpa Dan did not leave Crystal any instructions. He told Crystal and Noodle to go where the road leads them.

Crystal and Noodle began their next quest by walking by the Johnson's farm. Every day, Crystal walks by this farm and counts the brown cows in the pasture. Usually there are a group of ten cows that wander the large field and chew on grass. Today, Crystal noticed another cow in the distance standing separate from the other cows.

Crystal said to Noodle,

"Let's go say **hello** to the new cow."

Noodle is always ready to make new friends. With his tail already WAGGING, Noodle bounded over to the cow. Suddenly, Noodle stopped dead in his tracks. Crystal nearly fell over him.

"Holy cow!" Noodle exclaimed.

There, standing by a maple tree, was a black and white striped cow! It reminded Crystal of her favorite COOKIE. The cow was reading a book, but when she heard Crystal and Noodle approach, her *eyes* flew open wide.

The cow seemed anxious and NERVOUS.
Crystal quickly assured the cow,

"I'm so sorry we startled you.
We just wanted to come over and
introduce ourselves. I'm Crystal
and this is Noodle."

Not sure what to say, the cow softly *whispered*

"My name is Heather."

Both Crystal and Noodle had to lean in closer in order to
hear what Heather was saying.

"Why are you standing here all by
yourself? Don't you want to be with
the other cows?"

Crystal asked.

Heather looked rather sad and didn't respond. Noodle and Crystal sat down under the tree and noticed how peaceful it was there. There was a gentle *breeze,* and they could hear the leaves softly rustling in the trees. Crystal closed her eyes and felt the wind on her face. Nobody spoke, and Crystal wasn't sure what to say.

Finally Heather said,

"I don't like being with the other cows. They make fun of me and call me names because I'm

DIFFERENT.

They say I'm too sensitive and a cry baby. Then they say they're just kidding."

"That's not right!"

Crystal and Noodle exclaimed together.
Heather sighed and said,

"They don't **ACCEPT** me for who I am, and I don't think they ever will. And that's okay."

Noodle could not understand how others could be so mean, but Crystal could.

Heather found a shady spot next to Crystal and Noodle and settled on a cool patch of moss. She swatted FLIES with her tail.

She sat quietly for a few minutes, then shared,

"I like being alone. I like being someplace QUIET away from the noise. I like being me."

Noodle went over and sat right next to Heather.

"I like you, too,"

Noodle declared. Crystal noticed there were
tears in Heather's eyes.

Wanting to lessen Heather's sadness, Noodle abruptly
jumped up and started to 🎵 DANCE. Not only
did he wag his tail, he wagged his whole body! Laughing,
Heather jumped up too and started dancing with him.
Then Crystal started dancing. All three of them were
laughing and dancing around the maple tree.

Soon, they noticed a **BROWN** cow gradually moving toward them. Heather stopped in mid-dance. She was afraid the other cow would make fun of her.

Crystal noticed Heather was upset again and wanted to help. Crystal reached into her coat pocket to touch her beloved rocks, hesitated for a moment, and chose the perfect rock. Crystal presented the rock to Heather and said,

"I have a 🎁 GIFT for you, Heather.
This is a very special rock called
mookaite."

Noodle started laughing
UNCONTROLLABLY!

"You're giving a cow a rock called
MOO-kite? Seriously, MOO-kite!!"

Noodle said between giggles. Noodle was rolling
around on the ground laughing.

"Sometimes I get shy and NERVOUS
around other people and I'm not sure
how to talk to them."

Crystal said to Heather.

"Keep the rock near you and touch the
rock when you feel really anxious and
need CONFIDENCE. It really does
help. It works for me."

Heather was quite grateful for the present and for
Crystal's thoughtfulness.

Slowly, the brown cow approached them. Heather expected the brown cow to be disappointed with her or mean to her, but instead the cow ☺ SMILED at her with kindness. Cautiously, Heather smiled back.

"I saw you all dancing and it looked like fun,"

said the brown cow.

"The truth is I wanted to come here and tell you I'm sorry for how the other cows are treating you. I don't agree with how they treat you and I wanted to you know that."

Heather was shocked.

"Thank you. That means so much to me,"

Heather whispered.

As the brown cow turned to leave,
Heather bravely asked.

"Would you like to join us?"

The brown cow smiled, and the two started talking
and laughing. Crystal and Noodle waved goodbye, happy
that the two cows found a way to unite and start a
beautiful friendship.

HEATHER THE SENSITIVE COW

At first, seeing Heather made me sad. I felt so bad for her standing alone, away from the other group of cows, but after talking with her, I totally understand it.

I love being alone and spending time thinking, listening to music, and writing. I don't like being around a lot of people. It makes me tired and grouchy. I never thought anyone would understand me, but Heather does. I feel so much better knowing I'm not alone. Just like Heather, I feel bad when people make fun of me, saying I'm too sensitive and I take things too personally. It really hurts. If Heather can accept that she is different, so can I!

I was so nervous choosing the perfect gemstone for Heather. I was afraid I would pick the wrong one. Then I remembered what Grandpa Dan always says, "You'll just know.

Crystal's Journal

Use your intuition." The first time Grandpa
Dan told me about intuition, I had no idea
what he was talking about. He explained that
everyone has intuition and it is when you
just know something to be true. I never really
had an experience of that until today. I just
KNEW what gemstone Heather needed.
Woo Hoo!

MY THOUGHT FOR TODAY!
I wonder what it would be like to always use
my intuition. Any time I doubt that,

I let my doubt go!

Mookaite

HOW YOU SAY IT:

MOO-kite

Mookaite

CONFIDENCE

HOPE

COMMUNICATION

GEOLOGY FUN FACT

Some rocks when put under ultraviolet light change color. This process is called fluorescence.

MOOKAITE GEOGRAPHY

Mookaite Jasper is found only in Western Australia near Mooka Creek. Australia is the only country in the world that covers an entire continent. Australia has animals that are not seen anywhere else in the world, such as the platypus, kangaroo, and koala.

MOOKAITE HISTORY

The Australian Aborigines (the first people to live in Australia) used mookaite jasper as a healing stone for giving strength and energy.

WHAT DO I DO WITH MY ROCK?

Put it in your pocket, in your room, in your hand.

USE MOOKAITE WHEN YOU WANT TO:

be more confident,
have more hope,
tell people what you are thinking and feeling.

Mookaite is part of the jasper family of rocks. Other jasper rocks include: rainbow jasper, picture jasper, ocean jasper, and many more!

Crystal's Quest

To order a copy,
go to **LisaFontanella.com**
or **Amazon.com**

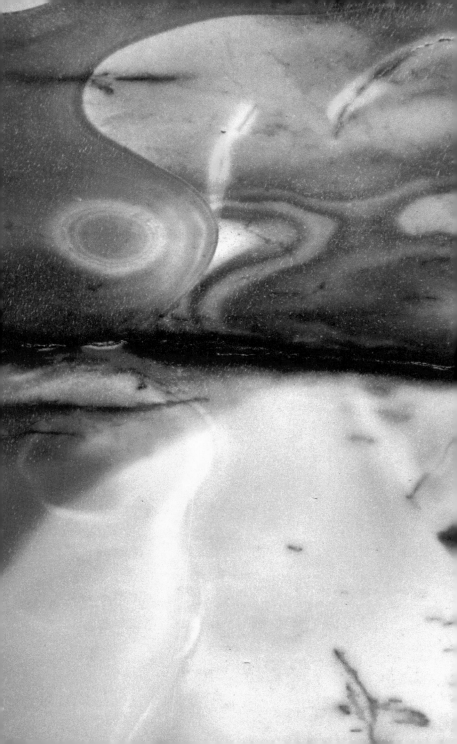

4
Chapter

INSIDE OUT

It was a GLOOMY afternoon, and the sky was filled with clouds. Potentially rainy weather didn't stop Crystal and Noodle from being excited about their next quest. However, Noodle was a bit less EXCITED than Crystal. If there's one thing Noodle hates even more than peas, it's getting wet!

Today, they were headed to one of Crystal's favorite places, a stream in the woods behind her house. Crystal loves watching the slow-moving stream and the turtles that live there.

As they walked to the stream, the sun started
to peek through the clouds.

"Maybe it will be a ☼SUNNY day after all,"

Crystal said to Noodle. This made Noodle's tail wag even
harder. Maybe he won't get wet after all!

When they arrived, four turtles were in the water
enjoying their swim. There was one smaller turtle
sitting on a rock on the edge of the stream.
She looked like she was sleeping.

"Good afternoon,"

Crystal said to the turtle, but the turtle did not respond.

Noodle, being curious, bent down in front of the
turtle so their NOSES were touching.

"Are you sleeping?"

Noodle asked loudly. The surprised turtle jumped.
Noodle jumped. Crystal laughed.

"I'm so sorry we bothered you,"

Crystal said, trying to contain her giggles.

"Noodle and I just wanted to say **hello.**"

"That's okay," said the turtle.

"I was deep in thought and didn't hear you. My name is Shelly."

"You look like you have a lot on your mind, Shelly. Can we HELP?"

Crystal asked. Shelly sighed and said,

"I just don't know what to do."

"Maybe if you tell us the problem, we can help," Crystal suggested.

The turtle sighed again and told
Crystal and Noodle her dilemma.

"I'm not a good swimmer,
and I don't like to swim."

Crystal and Noodle both looked CONFUSED,
so the turtle continued,

"All the other turtles keep asking me
to swim with them, but I really don't
want to. I love to lie on the rocks and
soak up the SUN."

Noodle nodded in understanding. Someone else who
doesn't like to get wet!

Shelly paused a moment then said,

"The other turtles DARE me to go
into the stream. I want them to like
me, but I don't want to be in the
water. What should I do?"

Crystal thought for a minute, reached into her pocket, and
pulled out a beautiful, white selenite rock. "

I keep this rock near me when I'm not
sure what to do. It always helps me make
my own decisions."

Crystal put the selenite rock next to the turtle.

"I have another 💡 idea," Crystal said.

"Grandpa Dan tells me that to figure out any problem, I need to ask myself what I want. Sometimes it's not the same as what everybody else wants and that's okay."

The turtle nodded in agreement.

"Grandpa Dan says the answers to all problems are inside of us. We just need to ask ourselves what's right for us."

The turtle thought about what Crystal said, then asked,

"You mean if I just go INSIDE myself, I can find the answer to my problem?"

"Exactly!" Crystal exclaimed.

"Excellent!" Shelly shouted.

Suddenly, the turtle's head
DISAPPEARED. Gone!

Noodle was stunned and very confused.
He 🔍 searched everywhere to find the turtle's
head but he couldn't locate it. Where did she go?

Crystal smiled and said,

"The turtle went inside her shell, Noodle. She's gone to find her answers."

Noodle wasn't sure if Crystal was teasing him so he bent
down to look inside the shell. Noodle poked his nose into
the opening in the shell, and the turtle's head
POPPED out!

Noodle **jumped.** Shelly and Crystal LAUGHED.

"It's time for us to go,
Noodle. We need to give Shelly
time alone to figure things out,"

Crystal said.

"Thank you both so much!"

Shelly exclaimed. Back into her shell she went.

Crystal and Noodle started walking away. Crystal turned
back and saw Shelly lying on a **rock** in the sun.

SHELLY THE TURTLE

Shelly is so sweet! I am so glad that Noodle and I met her. I know making decisions can be hard, especially when your decision might not be popular. ☹

Last year when I decided not to hang around with Sally anymore, it was really hard. She and I were good friends. BUT friends don't make you do things you don't want to do!!!!!!!! They don't make you feel bad about yourself.

That's not right!

I felt better after I talked to Grandpa Dan. He said he was proud of me for making a difficult decision. He reminded me that nobody should treat me badly.

That's not okay.

Crystal's Journal

I have friends now (and Noodle, of course)
who like me for me. 😃 I am HAPPY!

MY THOUGHT FOR TODAY!
I wonder what it would be like to always make
decisions that are right for me. Any time I
doubt that, I let my doubt go!

Selenite

HOW YOU SAY IT:
Sell-EN-ite

GEOLOGY FUN FACT
Meteorites are rocks from space that fall to the Earth and land on its surface.

SELENITE GEOGRAPHY
Selenite is found in many areas of the world, including Greece. Greece has ten national parks. The marine parks protect the endangered sea creatures, the monk seal, and the loggerhead turtle.

SELENITE HISTORY
Selenite was named after Selene, the Greek goddess of the moon.

The first Olympic Games were held in Greece in the city of Olympia in 700 B.C

WHAT DO I DO WITH MY ROCK?
Put it in your pocket, in your room, in your hand.

USE SELENITE WHEN YOU WANT TO:
make up your own mind,
believe in yourself,
be more confident.

There are many colors of Selenite: blue, green, orange, and peach. White is the most common color for Selenite.

Selenite

CONFIDENCE

BELIEVE IN YOURSELF

MAKE UP YOUR OWN MIND

Crystal's Quest
To order a copy,
go to **LisaFontanella.com**
or **Amazon.com**

Chapter 5

BEST FRIENDS

It was early morning, and the light was **peeking** through Crystal's window. Crystal stretched, so happy that today she was able to sleep in. She lay in bed, SMILING. That was until Noodle came bounding into her room, jumped on her bed, and gave her the slurpiest kisses ever!

"EEWWW!" Crystal screeched.

"It's Sunday morning, Noodle. I want to sleep in. Come back later."

Noodle is a wonderful dog, but he doesn't always do what he's told. Instead of letting Crystal go back to sleep, he jumped on the bed and began to pull the blankets off of her.

"NOODLE!!"

Crystal exclaimed. This made Noodle pull the blankets even faster.

Crystal tried to be mad, but Noodle had a goofy beagle grin and was doing a full body wag. He looked so

cute!

Shaking her head (and laughing), Crystal slowly got out of bed. Noodle could not contain his excitement. At first, Crystal couldn't figure out why Noodle was SO excited. Then she realized today was the day they were going to visit Noodle's best friend, Quackers.

Noodle and Quackers have been best friends for a
LONG time. Many people find it odd that a dog
and a duck can be best friends, but Noodle and
Quackers don't care.

They will be friends FOREVER

They quickly ate breakfast (the usual for Noodle), got
dressed, and started the quick walk to see Quackers.
Noodle was so excited, he practically ran the whole way.
Crystal was having trouble keeping up with him.

"Noodle, please slow down!"

Crystal pleaded. Noodle was DETERMINED and
did not stop or even slow down a little.

By the time they reached the small pond where
Quackers calls home, Crystal was gasping for breath.
That Noodle can really move when he wants to,
Crystal thought to herself.

As they approached the pond, Noodle let
out a huge AHH-OOOO to let Quackers know
he was there. Quackers did not come. Quackers
ALWAYS comes waddling at full *speed* when she knows
Noodle is around. Noodle waited anxiously to see his best
friend, but Quackers did not come.

Crystal and Noodle were both
confused and concerned.

They walked around the small pond and finally
found Quackers sitting under a TREE.

Noodle did a happy dance and let out another
AHH-OOOO. Crystal sighed with relief.

"I'm so glad to see you!"

Noodle exclaimed while **running** to Quackers.

Quackers said hello but stayed sitting. Quackers was
certainly not acting like herself today. Usually when she
sees Noodle, she runs up to greet him. Noodle wags his
tail and Quackers wags her tail feathers.

"Quackers, Are you OKAY?"

Crystal inquired.

"I guess so," Quackers said as she sighed.

"I'm just feeling rather
☹SAD and blue today."

Noodle looked BAFFLED. Quackers did not look blue to him. She looked white, just like always. Seeing Noodle's confusion, Crystal explained that Quackers was 'feeling blue' not that she actually turned blue. Noodle was relieved that his best friend was not changing color.

"Is there something wrong?"

Crystal asked.

"You can tell us. It might help to talk about it."

Noodle sat down next to his best friend with a worried look on his face.

Quackers sighed again.

"I don't know what's wrong with me. I don't want to do anything. I don't even go swimming much anymore."

As much as Noodle HATES getting wet,
Quackers LOVES it!

Noodle put his PAW around Quackers.
He didn't know what else to do.

Crystal reached into her jacket pocket
and pulled out a very special rock.

"This is an orange calcite rock,
Quackers. It really helps me when I
am feeling down and I don't know
why. I'd like you to have it."

Crystal put the rock next to Quackers.
Quackers was very grateful for her gift.

"I used to keep my feelings inside and
wouldn't talk about them to anyone,"

Crystal explained. "I was MISERABLE.

Quackers nodded in understanding.

"I realized that I wouldn't feel better
until I talked about how I was feeling.
So now I talk to Noodle and Grandpa
Dan, and I feel much better."

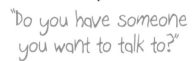

"Do you have someone
you want to talk to?"

Crystal asked. Quackers looked at Noodle,
her best friend in the whole world.

"Yes, I do," Quackers replied.

Noodle smiled and gave his beloved friend a **hug.**

"That's great!" Crystal said.

"Noodle is a good listener."

Crystal stood up to leave, saying,

"I'll leave you two alone to talk.
Anytime to you need us, we are both
here for you, Quackers."

Crystal leaned down, L♥VINGLY stroked
Quackers head, and slowly walked away.

"Thank you, Crystal,"

the duck said. Crystal turned back saying,

"You are most welcome. Anytime."

As Crystal walked away, she knew the courage it would
take for Quackers to share her feelings. With Noodle by
her side, Crystal knew Quackers was in GOOD hands.

QUACKERS THE DUCK

It was hard to see Quackers so sad and depressed. I really hope her talk with Noodle helped her. Noodle looked so upset. He is such a good friend.

If anybody can cheer Quackers up, it's Noodle!

Sometimes I still have trouble telling people how I feel. Sometimes I don't know how I feel. I just feel yucky and grouchy. I don't know why.

I was really nervous the first time I talked to Grandpa Dan about how I was feeling. He sat next to me, holding my hand, and he didn't interrupt me – not once! Grandpa Dan said that many people have times when they're sad or depressed, and it's important to tell someone how you feel.

Crystal's Journal

I didn't know other people get that way too.

Grandpa Dan was right. I felt so much better after our talk. Grandpa Dan is the BEST!

MY THOUGHT FOR TODAY!
I wonder what it would be like to always be comfortable sharing my feelings. Any time I doubt that, I let my doubt go!

Orange Calcite

Orange Cal-site

Orange Calcite

JOY

CONFIDENCE

CREATIVITY

GEOLOGY FUN FACT
The study of geology also includes studying the ocean floor.

ORANGE CALCITE GEOGRAPHY
Orange calcite is found in many areas in the world, including Brazil. Brazil is home to the Amazon Rainforest. There are many types (species) of plants and animals that live in this rainforest: around 1,300 bird species, 56,000 species of plants, 3,000 fish species, 430 mammal species and 651 reptile species. It has 2.5 million types of insects!

CALCITE HISTORY
Calcite is used to make chalk, marble, and limestone.

Limestone blocks were used in many of the pyramids of Egypt and Latin America.

WHAT DO I DO WITH MY ROCK?
Put it in your pocket, in your room, in your hand.

USE ORANGE CALCITE WHEN YOU WANT TO:
be happier,
be more confident,
be creative.

There are more than 4,000 different minerals.

Crystal's Quest

To order a copy,
go to **LisaFontanella.com**
or **Amazon.com**

CUT OUT BOOKMARK

Chapter 6

JUMP!

Crystal was especially excited today because they were going to visit the animals on the farm just up the road. Crystal's friend, Nathan, lives there. Nathan is a year older than Crystal and LOVES 🏒 **SPORTS!** All sports. His favorite now is hockey.

Nathan lives on a FARM that has many varieties of animals. On the farm, there are horses, chickens, sheep, goats, and the dreadful cats (according to Noodle). Noodle is not the bravest dog in the world. Cats scare him.

As they walked the long road leading to the farm, Noodle did his usual excited full body wag. He loves coming to the farm and visiting with *Nathan* and the animals! Also, Nathan gives him treats.

Noodle loves TREATS.

As they walked toward the white farm house, Nathan came over to meet them.

"Hi, Nathan," Crystal and Noodle said in greeting.

"I'm so happy you came
over to visit today,"

Nathan said enthusiastically.

"I have a very special treat
for you both."

Hearing the word treat, Noodle did his beagle happy
dance. Nathan laughed.

"I haven't forgotten you, Noodle.
Here's your treat."

SNARF!

Nathan led Crystal and Noodle to the field right next to
the red barn. As they approached the field, Crystal
couldn't believe what she was seeing. There was the
cutest goat she had ever seen!

"Meet **BANDIT**," introduced Nathan.

"Why do you call him Bandit?" Crystal asked.

Nathan smiled. "You'll see."

Crystal walked over to get a closer look.
She took off her backpack and laid it on the ground.
Kneeling down, she reached out to pet the goat.
In a flash, the goat had stolen her backpack!

Both Crystal and Noodle were stunned.

"Now I know why you call him Bandit.
He's one sneaky goat."

Crystal laughed.

Bandit jumped all over with the backpack in his mouth.

UP. DOWN. UP. DOWN. UP. DOWN. EVERYWHERE.

Crystal and Noodle  the goat,
but every time one of them got close,
the goat dashed away.

BACK. FORTH. UP. DOWN.

The energetic Bandit ran the length of the field and then
back again. Noodle made it his mission to recover Crystal's
backpack. He ran full speed after the goat.

Jump. Sprint. Jump. Run. Jump some more.
Bandit never stopped!

Noodle was determined to catch Bandit, but he was getting dizzy watching where the goat went.

LEFT. RIGHT.
ALL AROUND.

Noodle did his very best, but he couldn't keep up. Noodle wanted a nap.

Laughing, Nathan joined in and ran after Bandit. It took some time, but they finally grabbed the backpack.

Crystal, Nathan, and Noodle were EXHAUSTED but not Bandit! He was still jumping around.

"Are you always this active, Bandit?"

Crystal asked as she plopped on the ground. Nathan dropped down next to her. They all needed a nap.

"Yes, I am!" Bandit exclaimed.

JUMP.

JUMP.

Jump.

"I know I irritate the other goats, but I can't seem to STOP myself."

Crystal reached into her pocket to see which rocks she had brought. Nathan and Bandit curiously watched as she pulled the rocks out. Noodle was snoring.

Crystal thought for a second and handed
Bandit a black tourmaline rock.

"This will help you
relax and be calm."

Bandit looked at the rock then looked at Crystal.

"I doubt a rock is going
to help me relax,"

Bandit sighed as he jumped.

"When Crystal first told me about rocks
HELPING people, I thought
she was nuts,"

Nathan shared.

"But now I carry rocks
with me all the time."

Nathan reached into his pocket and pulled out three different
rocks: one blue, one green, and one brown.

"Give it a try," he said to Bandit.

Nathan and Crystal went to the house to find some
SNACKS. Nathan is always hungry, just like Noodle.

When they came back to the field, they both smiled.
There, SLEEPING side by side, were Noodle and
Bandit.

BANDIT THE GOAT

Boy, did Bandit make me laugh!!! I thought Noodle had a lot of energy, but Bandit has WAY more. I hope Bandit can calm down a bit and stop making the other goats mad. I know he can't help the way he is. Bandit really is very sweet (except for the stealing my backpack part).

I use black tourmaline when I'm a total spazz! I get anxious and upset, and I don't know what to do. I know I take things personally. That's who I am. Having tourmaline in my pocket all the time really helps. I was so surprised when Nathan said he believes rocks help people! He picked on me for years and thought I was crazy.

I'm happy he finally gets it.

Crystal's Journal

Noodle is sound asleep and I think he'll be snoring for a long time to come! He is one tired pooch! I'm one tired human! Off to bed.

MY THOUGHT FOR TODAY!
I wonder what it would be like to feel calm no matter what. Any time I doubt that,
I let my doubt go!

Black Tourmaline

HOW YOU SAY IT:
black TUR-ma-leen

Black Tourmaline

RELAXATION

COURAGE

PATIENCE

GEOLOGY FUN FACT
Gemstones are found all over the world, but did you know some are even found on other planets? The white gemstone Opal has been found on the planet Mars!

TOURMALINE GEOGRAPHY
Tourmaline is found in many areas in the world but was first discovered in the Unites States at Mount Mica in Paris, Maine. Maine is the most northern state in New England. Maine shares borders with the Canadian provinces of New Brunswick and Quebec.

TOURMALINE HISTORY
In 1820 in Paris Maine, two boys went exploring and discovered a green tourmaline stone. They searched the area and found more tourmaline stones in many colors. Tourmaline stones can be black, blue, green, pink, brown, yellow, and red.

WHAT DO I DO WITH MY ROCK?
Put it in your pocket, in your room, in your hand.

USE TOURMALINE WHEN YOU WANT TO:
relax,
have more courage,
be more patient.

Another name for Black Tourmaline is Schorl. Tourmaline is Maine's state mineral.

Crystal's Quest

To order a copy,
go to **LisaFontanella.com**
or **Amazon.com**

What new adventures lie ahead for Crystal and Noodle?

Will Noodle ever like peas?

Will the hyper squirrel ever stop interrupting people and learn to listen?

Find out in book two in the Crystal Series,

"Crystal Rocks."

You Rock!
JOURNAL AND COLORING BOOK:

A companion to the award-winning children's book, Crystal's Quest: An Adventure into the World of Gemstones

You ROCK! Journal and Coloring Book is designed to inspire creativity, self-expression and confidence in children ages 6 and up. This 108-page fun and inspirational children's journal includes doodle pages, coloring pages and lined journal pages.

Each journal page has encouraging quotes and writing prompts on topics such as mindfulness, self-acceptance and acceptance of others, sharing, doing what you love, feelings and emotions. The journal pages become an opportunity for kids to write down what they are feeling.

The black and white illustrations in the journal depict the beloved characters from the award-winning children's book, Crystal's Quest: An Adventure into the World of Gemstones. Readers will receive insightful and empowering encouragement from characters such as: Crystal, her beagle buddy Noodle, Squawk (a very loud parrot), Bandit the goat and more! The illustrations are perfect for the budding artist to color and make their own.

The journal can be used on its own or as a companion to the award-winning children's book, Crystal's Quest: An Adventure into the World of Gemstones.

Available at:

amazon.com   **BARNES**&**NOBLE**

CPSIA information can be obtained
at www.ICGtesting.com
Printed in the USA
BVHW021340110820
586103BV00018B/556

9 781641 840798